It is

Lola and her parents are walking
to the park to play.

They pass Lola's school and
her favourite shop,

The one where they bought
her brightly coloured top.

At the park, Lola runs around
smelling all of the flowers.

Roses, daffodils and tulips,
Lola could wander here for hours.

Suddenly, Lola hears someone
crying from behind a tree.

*"Mummy, Daddy, What is that
noise? Who could it be?"*

Together they take a peek,
and what do they see?

A little dragon! Sat all alone,
looking ever so lonely.

Mummy asks the little dragon,
"Whatever is wrong?"

The little dragon replies,
*"I am lost, and my mummy
and daddy are gone."*

"I was chasing butterflies,
but I think I ran too far.

Now I can't find my
mummy and daddy,
I don't know where they are."

Mummy says, *"Don't worry,
we will try to help you,*

*Finding your mummy and daddy
is what we will do."*

*"My name is Lola, and this is
my mummy and daddy."*

*"My name is Fee-Fee and thank you
for helping me."*

Lola holds out her hand and says,
"Come along with me,

We will find your mummy
and daddy, so come out from
behind the tree."

Fee-Fee holds Lola's hand as they
skip and hop through the park.

'I hope we find your parents soon
before it gets dark."

They look in the flower garden and
search down by the lake.

Lola says, *"Let's try the café, they
may have gone for tea and cake."*

"Not in there either, sobs Fee-Fee.
"I wonder where they could be?!"

Daddy assures her, *"It won't be long now,
you just wait and see."*

They have looked far and wide,
but Fee-Fee's mummy and daddy can't be found.

"I know!" shouts Lola excitedly,
"Let's try looking in the playground."

In a hurry, they run to the slides and swings.

"Mummy! Daddy!" Fee-Fee shouts
with a big smiley grin.

Thank goodness, Fee-Fee's mummy and daddy
have been found!

Everyone is so happy Fee-Fee is now safe and sound.

Fee-Fee runs over and gives her parents
a big kiss and cuddle.

Mummy dragon squeals, *"Where have you been?
We were in such a muddle!"*

Fee-Fee explains, *"I was chasing butterflies which were
flying high like a kite.*

*But when I turned around,
you were out of sight."*

"This is Lola who stopped
me feeling sad.

She is now the best friend
I have ever had."

Mummy dragon is happy,
"Thank you for your help Lola,
you are so kind."

"You are welcome" says Lola,
"I would never have left
Fee-Fee behind."

An excited Lola asks,
"*Can we all come to the park
together one day?*"

"*Oh yes please!*" says Fee-Fee,
"*I would love to come and play.*"

"*Ok,*" says mummy dragon,
"*Maybe next week we can spend
some time together?*"

"*What a wonderful idea*"
says Lola's mummy,
"*Let's hope for nice weather.*"

Fee-Fee waved goodbye and asked,
"Where will you be?"

Lola chuckled, "I think we should meet
at our new favourite tree!"

Lola and her parents set off home
after such an eventful day.

She cannot wait for her next trip to the park to play.

When the all arrive home,
Lola's tummy begins to rumble.

Mummy says, *"I think you deserve
some of my homemade
apple crumble."*

A smiling Lola says, *"Yummy,
yes please!
That would be such a treat."*

So as a family, they sit down at the
table ready to eat.

Suddenly, there is a knock at the door.

Daddy wonders, *"Who could that be?.*
Who could that be for?"

KNOCK
KNOCK

He opens the door, *"How strange,*
there is nobody around."

"Look!" says Lola, pointing to a shiny
pink present on the ground.

Lola asks excitedly, *"I wonder what's inside? Is it a gift for me?*

"Well," daddy replies, *"Let's open it at the table and then we will see."*

"The label says 'To Lola', so it must be a gift for you."

"YES!" says an excited Lola, *"I always love to get something new."*

To
Lola

Lola opens the gift, *"WOW! It is a beautiful princess dress!*

Covered in pink petals.
Who is it from?
Hmmm, I cannot guess."

Daddy looks inside the present,
"Well look what I have here!"

A note inside the box that will make all of this quite clear."

The note reads,

"Hello Lola,

Thank you so much for
your help today.

I can't wait to see you in
the park to play.

Lots of love, Fee-Fee"

Lola puts on the dress and
dances for the rest of the day.

Until mummy says,
*"Time for bed, please put the
princess dress away."*

Climbing into bed, Lola asks for a story
she has not heard before.

Mummy tells her about a princess and a little dragon,
who became best friends for evermore.

Now the story is finished, Lola
closes her eyes tight.

*"I love you mummy, daddy and
Fee-Fee."*

"I wish you all Good Night."

The End

Can you colour in
Lola and Fee-Fee?

For Francesca, for without her inspiration and wonderful imagination, this story would remain unwritten.

Lola
and the little,
Lost Dragon

Written by Marco Rossi (Daddy)

Inspired by the creative mind of Francesca Rossi (Daughter, aged 4)

Illustrated by: James Dimanarig

A word from Marco (Daddy)

This book was written during the spring/summer of 2020, at the peak of the Covid-19 pandemic. The reason I mention this, is because at a time of desperation, this period also gave me one the greatest gifts, spending every day with my 4-year-old daughter, Francesca.

We would visit the park everyday and she would gaze at all of the flowers and forage for leaves, petals and sticks to put in her nature bag. Francesca would also tell me stories from her imagination which was so wonderful to hear her creative mind at work.

This book was inspired by this daddy-daughter bonding and will be a positive legacy that we have taken out of this not so positive time in life.

We hope the book captures the loving sentiment that inspired the creation of the story (although we never found any dragons on our visits to the park!)

Enjoy Marco & Francesca

This storybook has been written to inspire kindness, helpfulness and friendships.